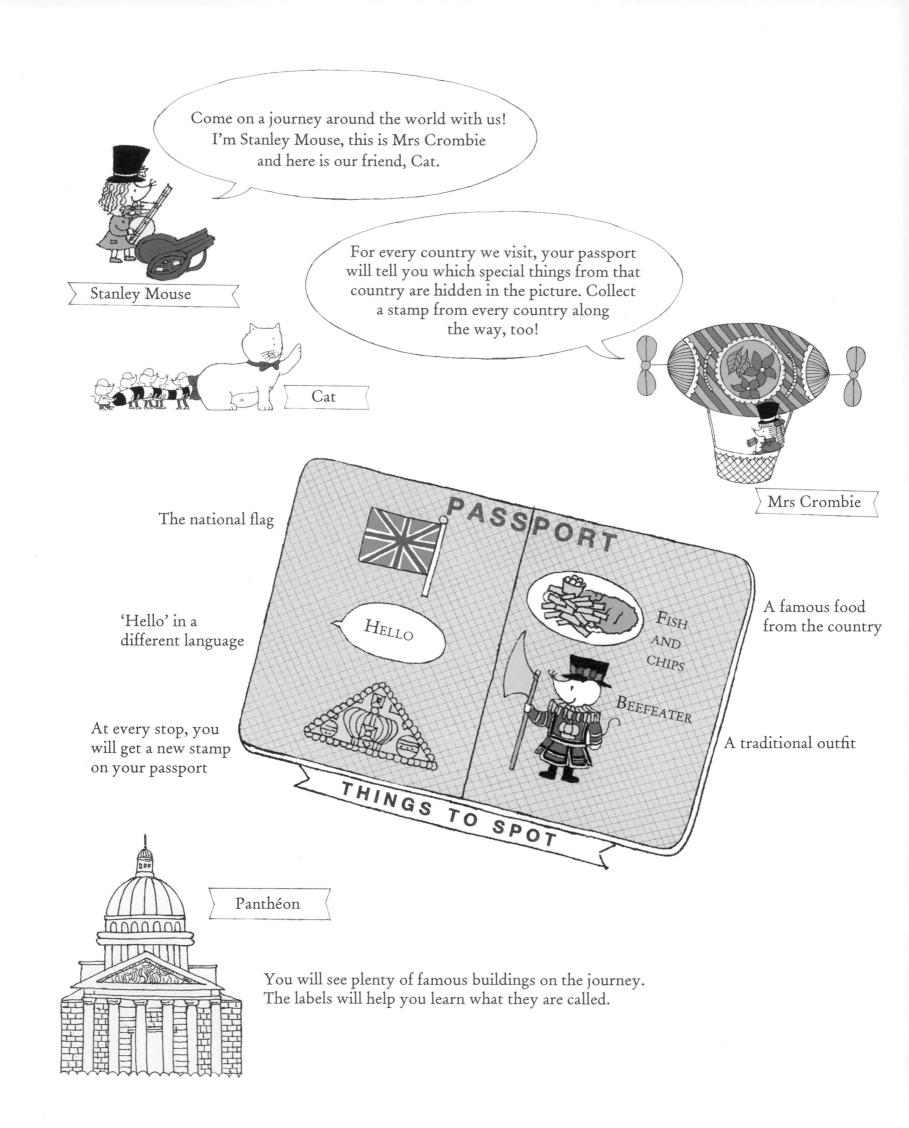

LONDON
UK

Stanley Mouse is a busker in Trafalgar Square.
Look beneath Nelson's Column, he always plays there.

Well, except for today, Pigeon's booked him a trip,
He'll be travelling onboard Mrs Crombie's Skyship.

MRS CROMBIE'S SKYSHIP

DEPARTS: LONDON   BOOKING CONFIRMED

The Shard

The Gherkin

Hello

He's packed cheese for a snack, and his banjo to play.
They are ready for take-off – 'Up, up, and away!'

Stanley asks Mrs Crombie 'Where's our first stop-off please?'
Mrs Crombie replies, 'Somewhere famous for cheese.'

PASSPORT

THINGS TO SPOT

Hello

FISH AND CHIPS

BEEFEATER

Big Ben

Westminster Abbey

The London Eye

Then she adds, 'My ship feels a bit heavy to me!'
Below deck, there is someone the mice cannot see.

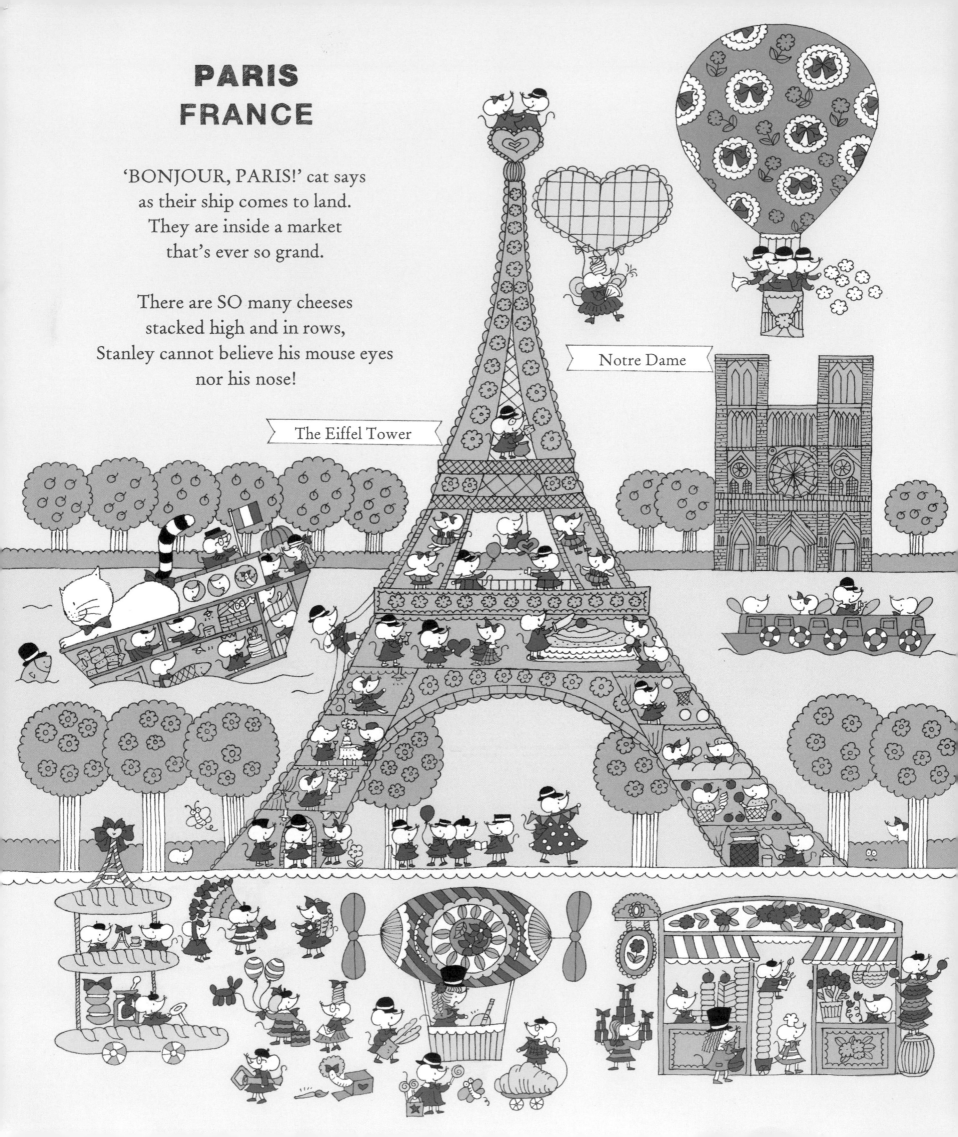

PARIS FRANCE

'BONJOUR, PARIS!' cat says
as their ship comes to land.
They are inside a market
that's ever so grand.

There are SO many cheeses
stacked high and in rows,
Stanley cannot believe his mouse eyes
nor his nose!

Notre Dame

The Eiffel Tower

He tries cheeses like Roquefort and Camembert, yummy.
But he soon eats too much and get pains in his tummy.

RIO DE JANEIRO BRAZIL

They see millions of mice all lining the streets,
they are dancing to Samba and Carimbó beats.
It is Carnival time here in Rio, Brazil,
and the rule is that no one's allowed to stand still.

Sugar Loaf Mountain

PASSPORT

Olá

Feijoada STEW

Baiana DRESS

THINGS TO SPOT

Santa Teresa Tram

Selaron's Steps

Stanley's hungry from dancing, the music's so loud!
So he looks for some cheese bread, away from the crowd.

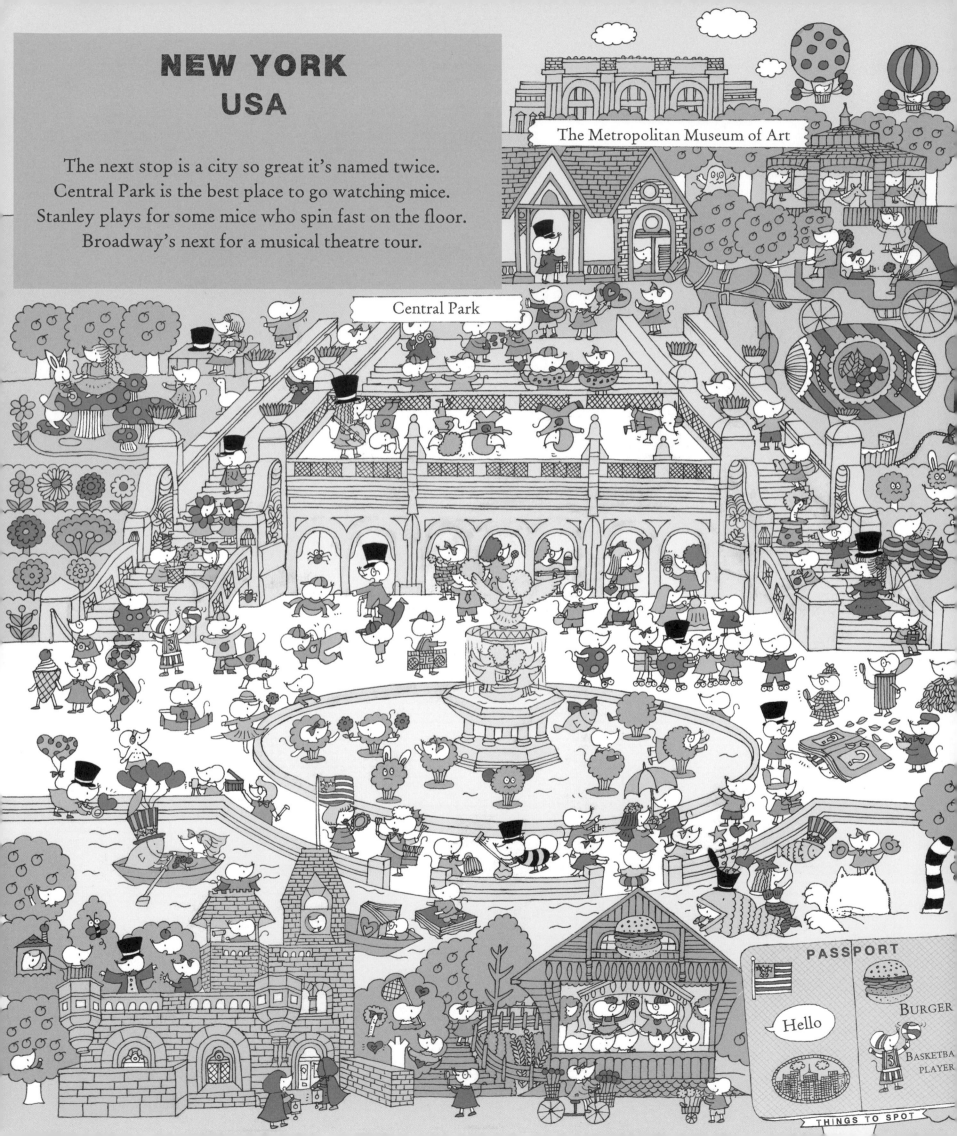

NEW YORK USA

The next stop is a city so great it's named twice.
Central Park is the best place to go watching mice.
Stanley plays for some mice who spin fast on the floor.
Broadway's next for a musical theatre tour.

The Metropolitan Museum of Art

Central Park

PASSPORT

Hello

BURGER

BASKETBALL PLAYER

THINGS TO SPOT

New Amsterdam Theatre

Then it's back to the ship. Stanley's late! He must run.
Can you guess what he's eating? It comes in a bun.

GREAT BARRIER REEF
AUSTRALIA

'G'day mate' squawks a very loud white cockatoo.
'Look below, there's a blue whale, she's waving at you.'
It's so hot in Oz, Stanley dives in for a swim.
There are all kinds of tropical fish around him.

G'day

BBQ

BUSHMAN

THINGS TO SPOT

Mrs Crombie can't see him,
so sends down a net.
'Come on, Stanley mouse,
and don't get my nice ship wet!'

BEIJING CHINA

'What is that, a big snake?' 'No! The Great Wall of China!
Of all famous walls in the world, none is finer.'
Stanley's hat blows right off in a big gust of air,
it blows on to Beijing so they follow it there.

Summer Palace

PASSPORT

Ni hao

DUCK PANCAKES

QIPAO DRESS

THINGS TO SPOT

Quanmen Main Street

Wangfujing Street

On a tower of mice sits a skilled acrobat.
He is juggling with something. It's Stanley's top hat!

ETOSHA NATIONAL PARK
NAMIBIA

Next a thrilling safari in Etosha Park.
You would not want to be here alone in the dark!
There are all kinds of animals out on the prowl.
What's that sound, look around,
did you hear something growl?

Alte Feste Fort

MOSCOW RUSSIA

From a very hot place
to a land full of snow.
A place known for bright, domed roofs,
it must be Moscow.

PASSPORT

Privet

HERRING UNDER A FUR COAT

SARAFAN PINAFORE

THINGS TO SPOT

St Basil's Cathedral

The Kremlin

Cathedral of Christ the Saviour

Stanley looks at the moon
through a huge telescope.
'If the moon's made of cheese
we'll go there next, I hope.'

'Not this trip, Stanley,
you'll need a Space Ship for that!
What's that under the basket,
a stowaway cat?'

Ostankino Tower

The Moscow Monorail

Moscow State University

Space Museum

Privet

TOKYO JAPAN

Cherry blossom and bright lights,
the next stop's Japan.
Cat heads straight off to eat
all the sushi he can.

Cocoon Tower

Roppongi Hills

Tokyo Tower

Metropolitan Government Build...

Akihabara

Konichiwa

PASSPORT

Konichiwa

SUSHI

SAMURAI

THINGS TO SPOT

Tokyo Skytree

Asakusa Tourist Centre

Senso-ji Temple

Nakimaste market

Tsukiji fish market

Simply follow your nose, this place sells every fish,
but the priciest type is Cat's favourite dish.
Uh oh, Cat has no money and stealing's a crime.
Can these two little mice stop this bad cat in time?

ROME
ITALY

They're in Rome now, on scooters, with ice creams – how nice! –
At Rome's huge Colosseum are gladiator mice.

The Colosseum

PASSPORT

Ciao

COLOMBA

GLADIATOR

THINGS TO SPOT

Stanley plays to the crowds at Rome's grand Trevi Fountain,
then they dine on spaghetti that's piled high like a mountain.
Then it's back to the Skyship to take a small doze.
Where they'll end up tomorrow, well, none of us knows!

The Trevi Fountain

Ciao

The Taj Mahal

PASSPORT

Namaste

THALI

SARI

THINGS TO SPOT

The mice zoom to the Taj with incredible speed,
wave to elephants and hope they don't cause a stampede!

BLACK FOREST
GERMANY

After the commotion they drift on the breeze
to Germany's Black Forest, and land in the trees.
They discover a castle owned by a mouse king
who invites them to hear the world's best mouse choir sing.

Neuschwanstein Castle

Guten tag

Eble Clock Park

PASSPORT

Guten tag

BRATWURST

LEDERHOSEN

THINGS TO SPOT

Then Cat finds an old clock shop, a wonderful thing,
Every hour all the clocks in the shop start to sing.

AMSTERDAM
THE NETHERLANDS

Over fields of bright tulips the three of them fly
'Ever been on a house boat? You really must try.'
Stanley gets out his banjo and plays as Cat steers,
and the crowds on the bridges eat cheese and shout 'cheers!'

There's a nasty storm due, Cat holds on with his claws.
It is blowing their ship further east and off course.

Damrak houses

PASSPORT

Hallo

STROOPWAFEL

LACE AND CLOGS

THINGS TO SPOT

SEOUL
REPUBLIC OF KOREA

Their poor Skyship's been blown straight into a tall tower.
Kind mice help unstick them but it takes them an hour.

N Seoul tower

Gyeongbok Palace

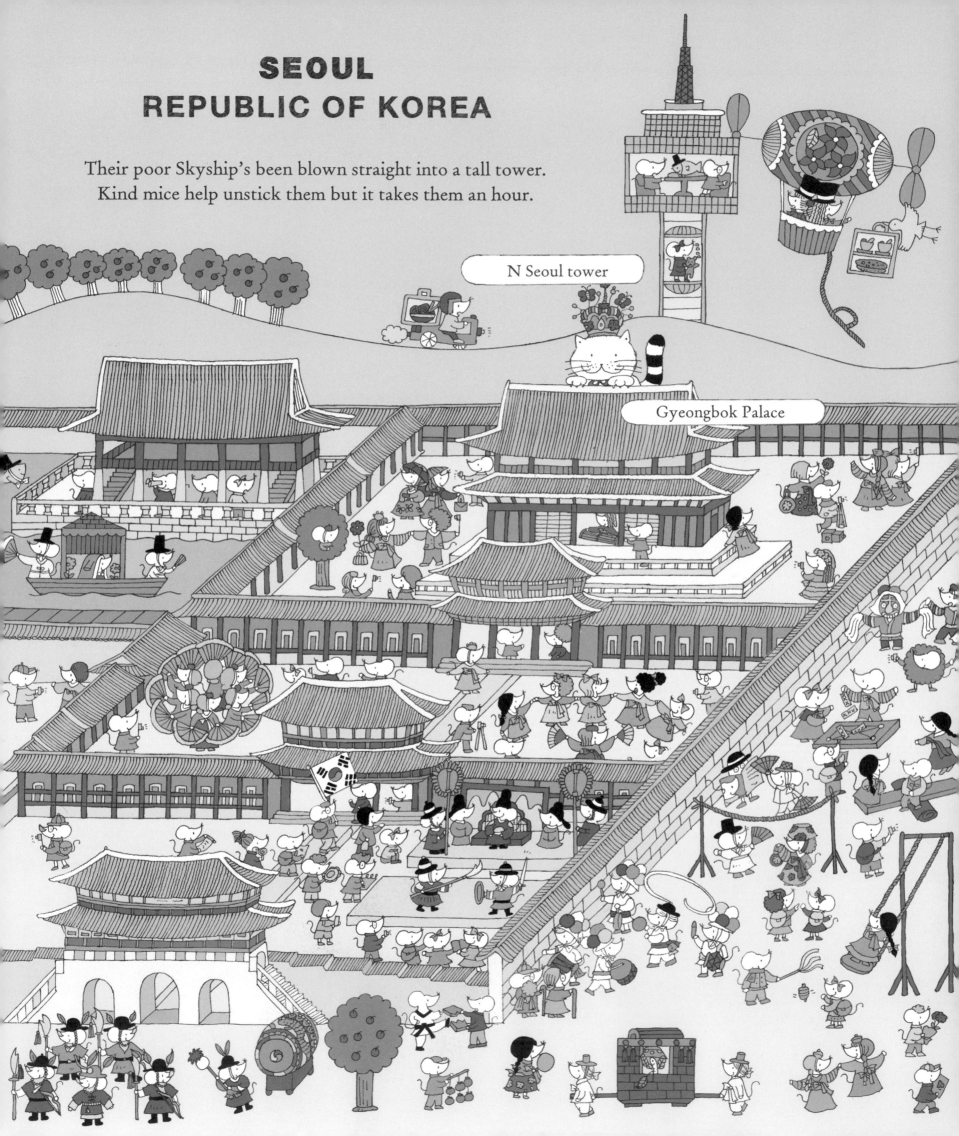

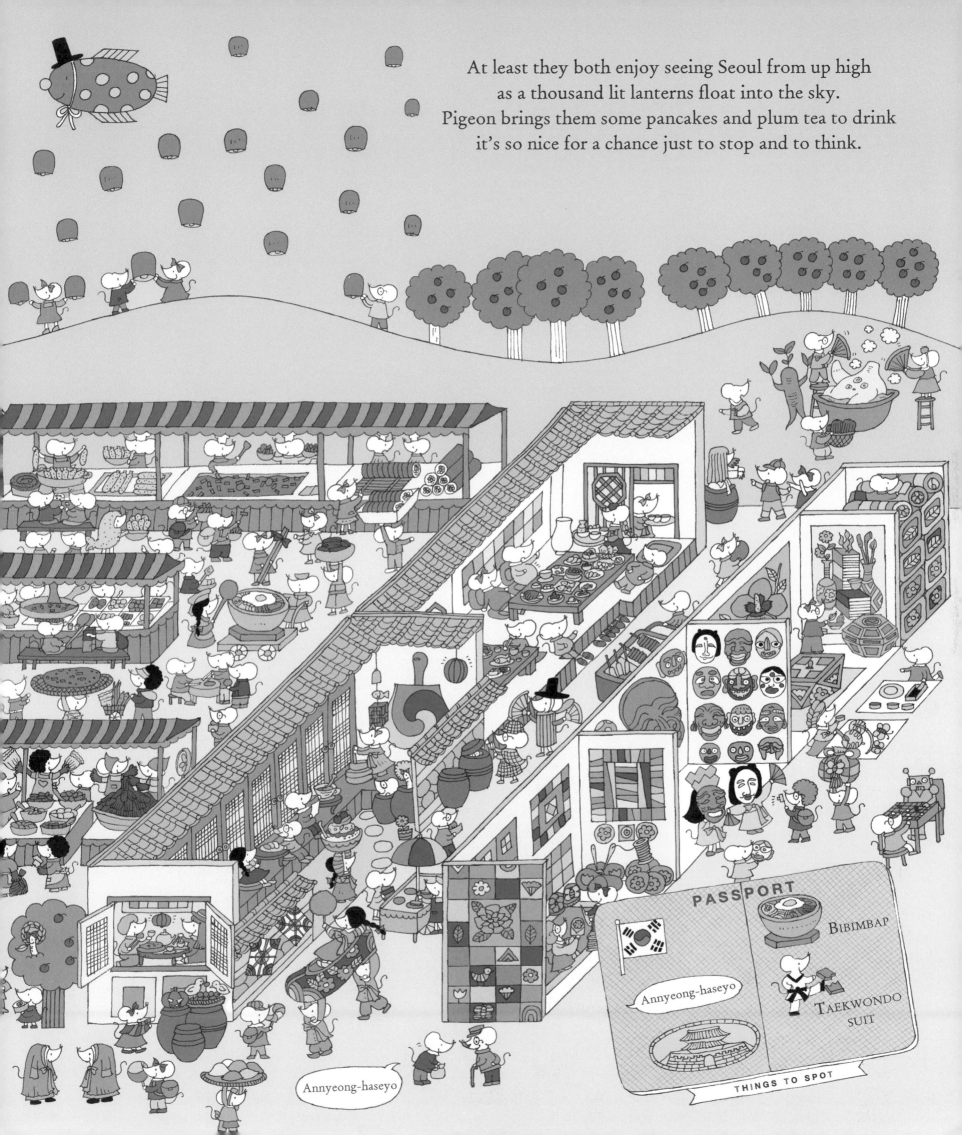

At least they both enjoy seeing Seoul from up high
as a thousand lit lanterns float into the sky.
Pigeon brings them some pancakes and plum tea to drink
it's so nice for a chance just to stop and to think.

BARCELONA SPAIN

Our last stop on the map is an inspiring place.
They meet hundreds of biker-mice, all here to race.

Park Güell

The Sagrada Família

PASSPORT

Hola

PAELLA

FLAMENCO DANCER

THINGS TO SPOT

Museu Nacional d'Art de Catalunya

The Magic Fountain of Montjuïc

In the evening they go to a big fountain show,
then Cat has to remind them, it's time they must go.

Hola

LONDON
UNITED KINGDOM

The Skyship touches back down in Trafalgar Square,
some familiar faces await them all there.
Stanley sings them new songs and shows snaps from his trip,
but he can't find his hat to take everyone's tip.

The National Gallery

Trafalgar Square

'Mrs Crombie,' he says, 'I've forgotten my hat!'
'I'll start up the ship.' she sings, 'Hop on board, Cat.'

St Martin-in-the-Fields

Nelson's Column

The Netherlands

UK

France

Spain

It[...]

USA

Mexico

Brazil

Namibia

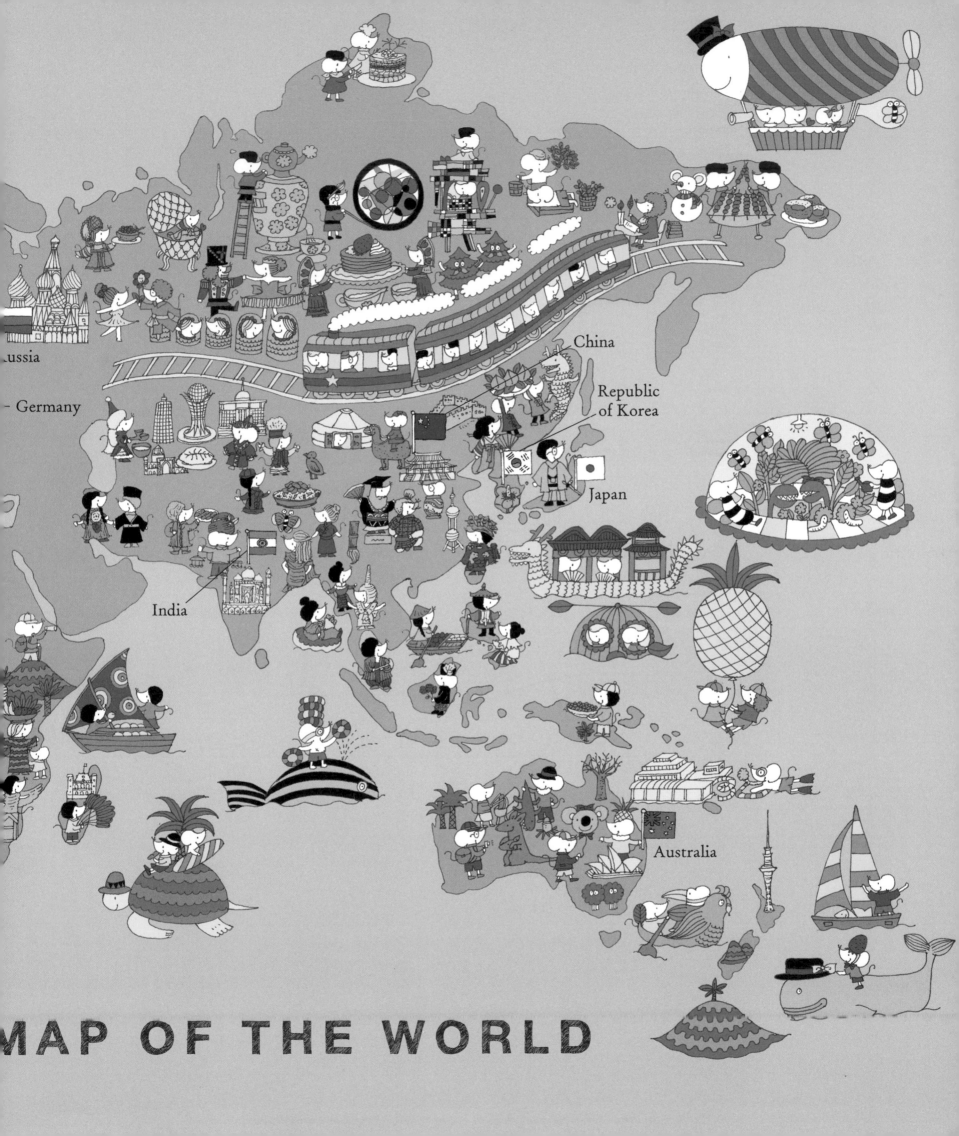

Russia

Germany

China

Republic
of Korea

Japan

India

Australia

MAP OF THE WORLD

Many thanks to God, my family and
friends, Roger Thorp, Lucy Brownridge,
Anna Ridley, Aaron Hayden and all
at Thames & Hudson. Special thanks
to Martin Salisbury, Pam Smy,
David Hughes and James Mayhew.

First published in the United Kingdom in 2018
by Thames & Hudson Ltd, 181A High Holborn,
London WC1V 7QX

Mice in the City: Around the World ©
2018 Thames & Hudson Ltd, London
Illustration © 2018 Ami Shin
Text © Jamie Harris

British Library Cataloguing-in-Publication Data
A catalogue record for this book is available from the British Library

ISBN 978-0-500-65152-0

Printed in China by RR Donnelley

To find out about all our publications, please visit **www.thamesandhudson.com**.
There you can subscribe to our e-newsletter, browse or download our
current catalogue, and buy any titles that are in print.